The Cotton boy

SALARIYA
BH
BOOK HOUSE

Principle 2

Chi... ...ghts

Beyond where the sun sets, there was a small kingdom called Cottonland. Everybody knew it as the White Kingdom, because it was full of cotton fields and flocks of sheep. The royal family was on the point of extinction, because King Ironhand and his wife were getting older and they still had no children.

4

Their luck changed with the birth
of their first and only son. He was very
small, with pale skin and hair so blond
that it was almost white.
'He is a very special child, but his health
is as delicate as cotton,' announced
one of the court astrologers.
'We must watch out for the signs,'
added another. 'Anything could make
him sick, even the sun's rays!'

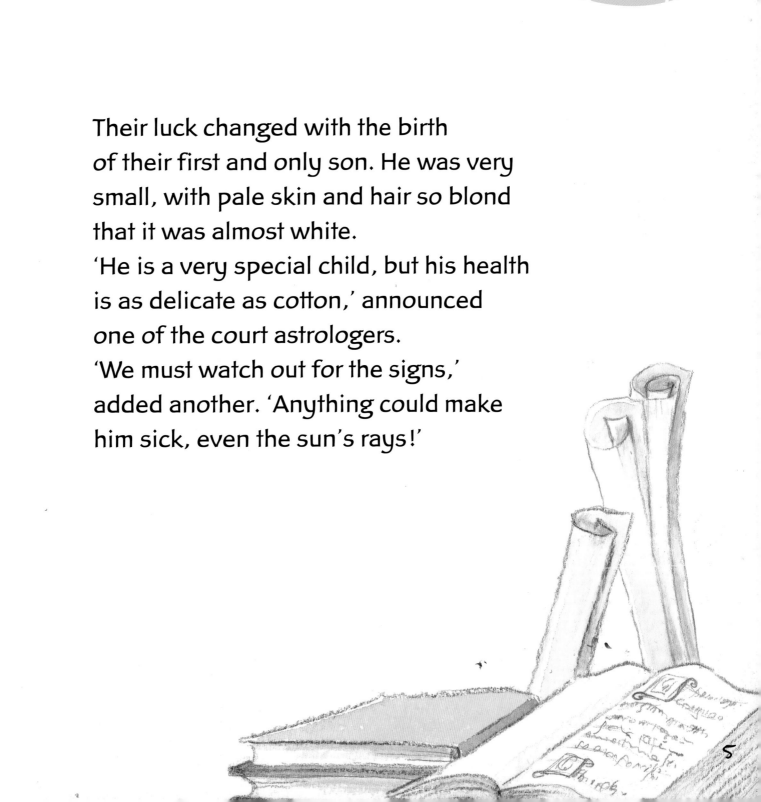

The king and queen wanted to protect their little prince, so they followed the astrologers' advice. The walls, floors, windows, furniture and all sharp objects were covered with soft cloth. 'Thick layers of wool and cotton must be used,' ordered King Ironhand; 'and use bright colours so that my son doesn't feel sad.'

8

The queen made every effort
to block off all the doors and
windows with stone and mortar.
This followed the astrologers'
second recommendation:
'He should only receive visitors
when it's absolutely necessary
and must never leave the palace.'
'Books are an open window to the
world,' said the queen. 'We will
hide them so that our little prince
can't see them. I don't want him to
be unhappy by seeing what he is
missing in the outside world.'

They had thought
of everything. But they
had forgotten that children
are restless and curious and that
people... talk. So, every time somebody
came to the palace, the prince hid and
listened to what each person had to say.
He always listened carefully and imagined
what the outside world might be like. And
little by little he imagined a world in which
the unimaginable was possible.

'I heard father say that letters were
flying in from all directions.
So... parcels and letters must have
wings,' he reasoned. 'Just like the
caged birds we have here in
the palace!'

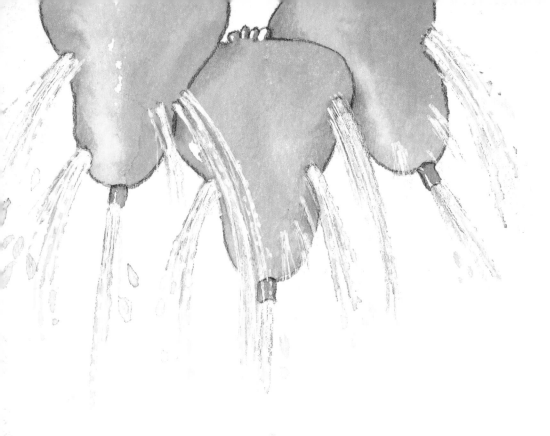

'Oh, girls, the market was just raining fruit today!'
laughed one of the cooks. 'Handfuls of strawberries!
Bright red cherries! And what juicy pears!'
The girls listened... and so did the little prince. He
imagined what it was like to see fruit raining down.

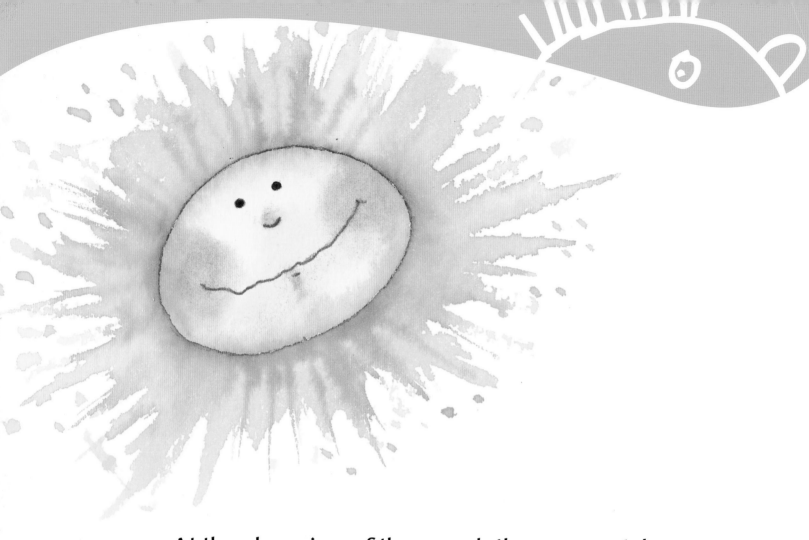

At the changing of the guard, the new watchman
was full of news of the village celebrations for
the Good Luck Festival:
'The meadow was full of children. You should
have seen them all diving into the water while
their parents were fishing and sunbathing.'
The prince had never seen a river. The only kind
of water he knew was... bath water!

'What are you carrying in that huge basket?' the prince asked the gardener.
'It's the grape harvest, little one. We're going to make wine, you'll see!'
The prince had never seen wine-making, so he could only guess what it was like.

It was the chimney sweep who surprised the
prince most. He was carrying a bundle of long
sticks and brushes. His face was covered with soot
and he was making a very strange noise.
'What's that noise?' asked the prince.
The sweep laughed: 'Have you never heard
anyone whistle before?'
He was right: the prince had never heard whistling.

The sweep explained that he was whistling a traditional winter tune.

'The country folk sing it all the time, and play fiddles and flutes to accompany it. Have you never heard this music before, either? Step closer to the chimney. Listen.'

23

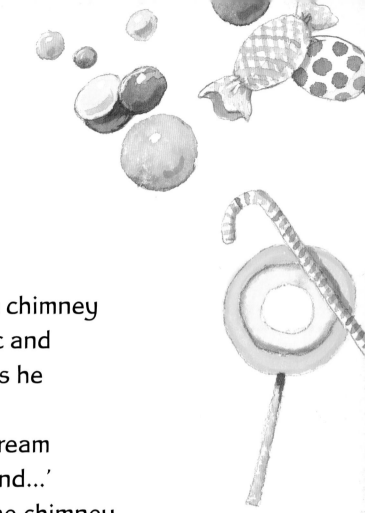

The prince came closer to the chimney and heard the sound of music and laughter. His nose twitched as he breathed in new smells, too.

'Mmm, the smell of spongy cream cakes, nuts, jam, chocolate and...'

The sweep disappeared up the chimney without finishing his sentence!

That was how the prince discovered how he could get out of the palace.
He hurriedly followed in the sweep's footsteps. With great curiosity and excitement, he climbed up the dark chimney as it got narrower and narrower. When he reached the top, he stopped to rest – and the wind touched his cheek for the first time.

'Hurry, hurry, guards!
Open the doors!' ordered
the king when he heard
his son's laughter outside.
His mother saw the
footprints in the snow
and shouted anxiously:
'The sun! Get out of the
sun, and come away from
the other children!'

The prince heard none of these warnings as he laughed and played in the snow. The king and queen now saw that their astrologers had been wrong – the young prince was as healthy as any other child.

Only one thing had changed: he was happy!

Principle 2

of Children's Rights:

The child shall enjoy special protection, and shall be given opportunities and facilities, by law and by other means, to enable him or her to develop physically, mentally, morally, spiritually and socially in a healthy and normal manner and in conditions of freedom and dignity. In the enactment of laws for this purpose, the best interests of the child shall be the paramount consideration.

The prince in the story suffered from excessive protection. The king and queen wanted to protect him from the slightest danger and ended up isolating him from everything. They didn't realise that they were being selfish. Their fear and ignorance had made them restrict their son's freedom, which led him to create an imaginary world.

Unwittingly, they had created a situation contrary to that proclaimed in the Rights of the Child, because without access to culture or human contact, the prince did not have the same opportunities as other children.

Children's Rights

Adopted by the General Assembly of the United Nations in Resolution 1386 (XIV) of 10 December 1959.

PREAMBLE

I. *Whereas* the peoples of the United Nations have, in the Charter, reaffirmed their faith in fundamental human rights and in the dignity and worth of the human person, and have determined to promote social progress and better standards of life in larger freedom,

II. *Whereas* the United Nations has, in the Universal Declaration of Human Rights, proclaimed that everyone is entitled to all the rights and freedoms set forth therein, without distinction of any kind, such as race, colour, sex, language, religion, political or other opinion, national or social origin, property, birth or other status,

III. *Whereas* the child, by reason of his physical and mental immaturity, needs special safeguards and care, including appropriate legal protection, before as well as after birth,

IV. *Whereas* the need for such special safeguards has been stated in the Geneva Declaration of the Rights of the Child of 1924, and recognised in the Universal Declaration of Human Rights and in the statutes of specialised agencies and international organisations concerned with the welfare of children,

V. *Whereas* mankind owes to the child the best it has to give,

VI. Now, therefore, *The General Assembly* proclaims this Declaration of the Rights of the Child to the end that he may have a happy childhood and enjoy for his own good and for the good of society the rights and freedoms herein set forth, and calls upon parents, upon men and women as individuals. And upon voluntary organisations, local authorities and national Governments to recognise these rights and strive for their observance by legislative and other measures progressively taken in accordance with the following principles:

Principle 1
The child shall enjoy all the rights set forth in this Declaration. Every child, without any exception whatsoever, shall be entitled to these rights, without distinction or discrimination on account of race, colour, sex, language, religion, political or other opinion, national or social origin, property, birth or other status, whether of himself or of his family.

Principle 2
The child shall enjoy special protection, and shall be given opportunities and facilities, by law and by other means, to enable him to develop physically, mentally, morally, spiritually and socially in a healthy and normal manner and in conditions of freedom and dignity. In the enactment of laws for this purpose, the best interests of the child shall be the paramount consideration.

Principle 3
The child shall be entitled from his birth to a name and a nationality.

Principle 4
The child shall enjoy the benefits of social security. He shall be entitled to grow and develop in health; to this end, special care and protection shall be provided both to him and to his mother, including adequate pre-natal and post-natal care.

The child shall have the right to adequate nutrition, housing, recreation and medical services.

Principle 5
The child who is physically, mentally or socially handicapped shall be given the special treatment, education and care required by his particular condition.

Principle 6
The child, for the full and harmonious development of his personality, needs love and understanding. He shall, wherever possible, grow up in the care and under the responsibility of his parents, and, in any case, in an atmosphere of affection and of moral and material security; a child of tender years shall not, save in exceptional circumstances, be separated from his mother. Society and the public authorities shall have the duty to extend particular care to children without a family and to those without adequate means of support. Payment of State and other assistance towards the maintenance of children of large families is desirable.

Principle 7
The child is entitled to receive education, which shall be free and compulsory, at least in the elementary stages. He shall be given an education which will promote his general culture, and enable him, on a basis of equal opportunity, to develop his abilities, his individual judgement, and his sense of moral and social responsibility, and to become a useful member of society.

The best interests of the child shall be the guiding principle of those responsible for his education and guidance; that responsibility lies in the first place with his parents.

The child shall have full opportunity for play and recreation, which should be directed to the same purposes as education; society and the public authorities shall endeavour to promote the enjoyment of this right.

Principle 8
The child shall in all circumstances be among the first to receive protection and relief.

Principle 9
The child shall be protected against all forms of neglect, cruelty and exploitation. He shall not be the subject of traffic, in any form.

The child shall not be admitted to employment before an appropriate minimum age; he shall in no case be caused or permitted to engage in any occupation or employment which would prejudice his health or education, or interfere with his physical, mental or moral development.

Principle 10
The child shall be protected from practices which may foster racial, religious and any other form of discrimination. He shall be brought up in a spirit of understanding, tolerance, friendship among peoples, peace and universal brotherhood, and in full consciousness that his energy and talents should be devoted to the service of his fellow men.

Visit our **new** online shop at
shop.salariya.com
for great offers, gift ideas, all our new
releases and free postage and packaging.

Published in Great Britain in MMXIII by
Book House, an imprint of
The Salariya Book Company Ltd
25 Marlborough Place, Brighton BN1 1UB
www.salariya.com
www.book-house.co.uk

1 3 5 7 9 8 6 4 2

A CIP catalogue record for this book is available from the British Library.

Printed and bound in China.

PB ISBN: 978-1-908973-27-6